Five Short Plays

by Adam Szymkowicz

The Plays:

Berbert

Three Cheerleaders Cheering for the Worst Team in the History of High School Sports

The Funeral

Snow

Golden Town

Berbert
Copyright © 2019, Adam Szymkowicz

Seth Glewen
The Gersh Agency
41 Madison Avenue 33rd Floor
New York, NY 10010
P: 212-997-1818
F: 212-391-8459
sglewen@gershny.com

SPECIAL NOTE

Anyone receiving permission to produce Berbert is required to give all credit to the Author as sole and exclusive Author of the Play on the title page of all programs distributed in connection with performances of the Play and in all instances in which the title of the Play appears for purposes of advertising, publicizing, or otherwise exploiting the Play and/or a production thereof. The name of the Author must appear on a separate line, in which no other name appears, immediately beneath the title and in size of type equal to 50% of the size of the largest, most prominent letter used for the title of the Play. No person, firm, or entity may receive credit larger or more prominent than that of the Author.

BERBERT
by Adam Szymkowicz

Loosely based on The Book of Titus, commissioned by Spark and
Echo.

CAST of CHARACTERS:

ANGIE, female
T, female
PAUL, male
BERBERT, non-binary

SETTING:

T's Office

TIME:

The Present

1

(Lights up on ANGIE and T in mid conversation.)

T
Okay, then.

ANGIE
But Paul wants to talk to you first.

T
I don't want to.

ANGIE
You have to. You know he likes to give advice. And he's still the boss.

T
He's here?

ANGIE
He'll be here in a minute.

T
He won't understand.

ANGIE
No, but--

T
I should try?

ANGIE
What else are you gonna do?

T
What do I say?

ANGIE
You'll think of something.

2.

(Transition. ANGIE has left. PAUL is there.)

T
Paul, I fell in love.

PAUL
You what?

T
I fell--

PAUL
I heard you. That's not what was supposed to happen.

T
I know. I know.

PAUL
I sent you here to hire a new staff.

T
I know.

PAUL
And you--

T
Yeah. Fell in love.

PAUL
But what about the hiring?

T
I'm still going to do that. I'll totally do that. But I have to talk to
HR because I'm in love with one of them.

PAUL
I gave you clear instructions.

T
I know.

PAUL
And none of this was in the hiring manual.

T
I want you to meet them.

PAUL
Who?

T
The person I fell in love with.

PAUL
I'm not gonna wait around. I'm not gonna--

T
We're having lunch. You can join us.

3.

(Transition. They have lunch. BERBERT is with them.)

T
Paul, I want you to meet Berbert.

PAUL
Nice to--

BERBERT
Berbert.

PAUL
T speaks very highly of you.

BERBERT
Berbert.

PAUL
Does he--

T
No. All they say is "Berbert."

PAUL
And this is the one you're in love with?

T
Yeah. Look into Berbert's eyes.

BERBERT
Berbert.

PAUL
Yes, they are very soulful.

T
Right?

PAUL
But--Maybe someone else, a little more--

T
Love does not put on airs!! You said that.

PAUL
I know, but you're taking it out of context.

T
Are you envying? Don't envy.

PAUL
I'm not. I mean I'm trying not to.

T
Don't be hurt. I want you to bless my love with Berbert.

BERBERT
Berbert.

T
Before Berbert I was wicked, foolish, disobedient, deceived,
serving various lusts and pleasures, living in malice and envy
hateful and hating. But no longer. Berbert makes me a better
person. Makes me good. Makes me whole. I can sing now. I can
taste things. Food tastes amazing. I was in a hole with no light, no
hope and then Berbert looked at me and now--

BERBERT
Berbert.

T
I'm full of love now for everyone. Berbert fills my cup over.

PAUL
Okay, well I guess I'm happy, it's just-- I thought you and me
would have a go of it one day.

T
Sure. Yeah.

PAUL
So.

T
I thought that too. I did. But you were always out of town and you
know, HR would frown upon it.

PAUL
HR would frown upon this!

BERBERT
Berbert.

T
Thank you for being happy for me.

PAUL
I don't know that that's true.

T
Well thank you for pretending. And thanks for coming down to the
office. And for smoothing it over with HR.

PAUL
Oh you want me to--

T
Berbert and I really appreciate it.

BERBERT
Berbert.

PAUL
Look, I'm going to do the right thing here. I'm going to be
generous and kind about this but before we move on, are you sure,
like really sure, like absotively sure that you and me--

T
I'm sure. Maybe before. But not now. Because--

BERBERT
Berbert.

PAUL
And you're sure that he--

T
There were impeccable references both for Berbert as a human and
as an employee. Everyone loves and respects Berbert. And no one
has ever treated me better.

PAUL
I see.

BERBERT
Berbert.

T
What's that?

BERBERT
Berbert.

T
Berbert has something to say.

BERBERT
Berbert.

T
He's listening.

PAUL
Yes.

T
We're both listening.

BERBERT
Berbert berbert berbert ber-bert berbert berbert. Berbert berbert.
Berbert berbert berbert berbert berbert berbert berbert berbert
berbert berbert berbert berbert berbert berbert berbert berbert
berbert berbert berbert berbert berbert berbert berbert berbert
berbert berbert. Berbert.

T
Well.

PAUL
I guess there's nothing more to say.

BERBERT
Berbert.

(END OF PLAY)

Seth Glewen
The Gersh Agency
41 Madison Avenue 33rd Floor
New York, NY 10010
P: 212-997-1818
F: 212-391-8459
sglewen@gershny.com

SPECIAL NOTE

Anyone receiving permission to produce Three Cheerleaders
Cheering for the Worst Team in the History of High School Sports
is required to give all credit to the Author as sole and exclusive
Author of the Play on the title page of all programs distributed in
connection with performances of the Play and in all instances in
which the title of the Play appears for purposes of advertising,
publicizing, or otherwise exploiting the Play and/or a production
thereof. The name of the Author must appear on a separate line, in
which no other name appears, immediately beneath the title and in
size of type equal to 50% of the size of the largest, most prominent
letter used for the title of the Play. No person, firm, or entity may
receive credit larger or more prominent than that of the Author.

Three Cheerleaders Cheering for the Worst Team in the History of
High School Sports
by Adam Szymkowicz

PETER
JENNIFER A
JENNIFER X

1

*A field. PETER, JENNIFER A and JENNIFER X stand around,
perhaps eating junk food. They are all dressed in cheerleader
outfits. Peter's outfit is similar but fashioned for a male
cheerleader. They may practice cheers stylistically perhaps
silently between scenes but right now they are not cheering at all.
They half watch the game, bored, then:*

                              JENNIFER A

Racism is so wrong!

                                        *(JENNIFER A and
                                        JENNIFER X laugh. PETER joins
                                        in after a while)*

                              JENNIFER A

I'm totally against racism.

                              JENNIFER X

I know it, me too, right?

JENNIFER A

There's like nothing worse. I'm serious. If I see someone who's being racist, I want to be like hey you, you racist, I see you being racist and I think you should stop your racism.

JENNIFER X

You should totally do that.

JENNIFER A

Fucking racists!

JENNIFER X

I know it.

JENNIFER A

Peter, aren't you against racism?

JENNIFER X

Peter?

JENNIFER A

Peter, I'm going to beat you up unless you say you're against racism too.

(PETER chuckles)

JENNIFER A

No, you know what I'm going to do? I'm going to rub my sweaty crotch all over your face.

(PETER chuckles.)

JENNIFER A

No seriously. I mean it.

JENNIFER X

She's totally serious.

JENNIFER A

Jennifer will hold you down and I am going to rub my meaty
sweaty crotch all over your face until you suffocate or get a boner,
whichever comes first. That's not what you want, is it, Peter?

JENNIFER X

Is it, Peter?

(PETER stops chuckling,
looks concerned.   A beat. Then,
the JENNIFERs laugh.   PETER
laughs too, nervously.)

JENNIFER A

Oh, Peter, you're a fucking riot.

JENNIFER X

He really is.

2

(The JENNIFERS are
smoking. PETER watches.)

JENNIFER X

No, you have to hold it like this.

JENNIFER A

I am.

JENNIFER X

And then you inhale like this. You have to inhale and then you
blow it out but sort of pouty so it's sexy.

JENNIFER A

How's this?

JENNIFER X

That's good.

JENNIFER A

I want to look very sexy. Do I look very sexy?

JENNIFER X

You look sexy.

JENNIFER A

I want to look very sexy.

JENNIFER X

How do I look?

JENNIFER A

Good. More disdain. You have to look at everyone like no one is in any way interesting. Don't even look. You care so little you don't even look really. Yeah, like that. That's good.

JENNIFER X

You look good. Stick out your butt more.

JENNIFER A

Like this?

JENNIFER X

Yeah. Very sexy. Peter, don't we look sexy?

(PETER looks away
embarrassed. JENNIFER A
laughs.)

JENNIFER
(scary)

Look! Peter, Look at me! Look at me! I will force you to see me.

(PETER looks at her.)

                                        JENNIFER A
You know what I'm for, you guys? Hey! Guys! Guys! I am
totally for freedom!

                                        (JENNIFERS laugh. PETER
joins them.)

                                        JENNIFER A
But I mean it. Freedom is so important.

                                        JENNIFER X
I know.

                                        JENNIFER A
It's like so important, that I think some people should have less of
it so other people like us get more.

                                        JENNIFER X
I know right.

                                        (They laugh)

                                        JENNIFER A
People should die for my freedom.

                                        JENNIFER X
I know it.

                                        JENNIFER A
Peter, you'd die for our freedom, wouldn't you?

                                        JENNIFER X
Wouldn't you, Peter?

You want us to be free, don't you Peter?

Say you'd die for our freedom, Peter.

JENNIFER A

Say it!

JENNIFER X

Say it!

JENNIFER A

Say it!

(They laugh)

JENNIFER X

Oh, Peter. Why can't you be romantic?

JENNIFER A

Yeah, why can't you?

JENNIFER X

You know, I would probably go down on Peter if he was romantic.

JENNIFER A

It's a shame.

JENNIFER X

Yeah. When I suck cock, I go all the way down to the pubes.

JENNIFER A

Did you hear that, Peter?

JENNIFER X

Peter, did you hear that?

(Pause)

PETER

I just think, when you love someone, then maybe . . . that's when
you do things with them . . . like those things . . . I'm just waiting
for that person to show up, but I just don't know when that will
happen. It seems like it never will. And I want it to so bad, but it's
like I don't belong here. Everyone just stares at me as if to say
"what are you doing here?" and I don't know what I'm doing here.
At all. I just hope someday there will be someone who will look at
me and see my value and say "yeah, you and me, we're the same."
Cause no one around here is like me. And I'm not even sure why.
Sometimes I just feel like there's no point in saying anything
anymore because when I do, no one understands what I'm saying.
We're all speaking the same language but I'm on a different
frequency or something. I don't know.

(Silence.)

JENNIFER A

Well—

JENNIFER X

I mean—

JENNIFER A

I'm glad you're here, Peter.

JENNIFER X

Yeah, me too.

JENNIFER A

Now tell me you're going to die for our freedom or I'll suck your
cock.

(They laugh) (lights)

sglewen@gershny.com

The Funeral
by Adam Szymkowicz

MICHAEL
LISA

Scene 1

(Living room of an Apartment. MICHAEL is packing a box. LISA comes into the room, looks at MICHAEL and exits without a word.)

MICHAEL
Is this yours? This book, is it—Lisa!—I'm putting it in the box.

(MICHAEL puts it in the box.)

(LISA reenters.)

LISA
What did you say?

MICHAEL
Nothing.

LISA
Did you—

MICHAEL
Forget it.

LISA
That's mine.

(LISA takes the book out of the box and exits again.)

MICHAEL
I thought you weren't going to be here. You said you wouldn't be here.

LISA
(off)
I wasn't going to be here. *(entering)* But I'm here now. So.

(LISA exits again.)

MICHAEL
Oh, God. How did this happen?

LISA
(off)
What?

MICHAEL
I said "What happened?" To us.

(LISA reenters)

LISA
Let's not have this conversation.

(LISA exits)

MICHAEL
We're just never going to talk about it? Is that fair?

LISA
(entering)
Now you're talking about "fair?" What do you want from me?

MICHAEL
I don't know.

LISA
You want to have a funeral for our relationship?

MICHAEL
A—

LISA
You want to say goodbye to our relationship in a formal way?

MICHAEL
Um—

LISA
Or are you just looking for post relationship sex?

MICHAEL
Are we already post relationship?

LISA
You tell me. You're the one packing the box.

MICHAEL
You don't want me to leave?

LISA
I didn't say that. Stop putting words in my mouth.

(A pause. They look at each other.)

MICHAEL
OK. Let's do it. Let's have a funeral for our relationship.

LISA
I'll dim the lights.

(She does.)

LISA
Do you want to start?

MICHAEL
No, no, you go ahead.

LISA
You sure?

MICHAEL
Please.

LISA
Dearly beloved. We are gathered here in the sight of God to mourn
the death of our relationship. It . . . It was a good relationship.

MICHAEL
It was.

LISA
It wasn't perfect. No one is. I mean sometimes —

MICHAEL
Let's not speak ill of the dead.

LISA
It brought all of us here a great deal of joy for a long time. Pain
too. It brought us pain.

(MICHAEL clears his throat)

LISA
But we try to remember the joy. We don't need to talk about you
and Janie Millner.

MICHAEL
Nothing happened!

LISA
Or the way you belittle my sport socks.

MICHAEL
I'm not apologizing for that.

LISA
The tiny insults, the painful hurts, the slights, the times you
ignored me. Or your wrestling programs.

MICHAEL
I though you liked my wrestling programs.

LISA
No, we will talk about the good times. Hold on.

(LISA exits)

MICHAEL
You watched it with me. Don't pretend you don't like wrestling all of a sudden.

(LISA reenters carrying a box.)

LISA
Here's something we can bury.

MICHAEL
What's this?

LISA
Our relationship. *(Takes a napkin out)* From our first date.

MICHAEL
Oh. You kept it.

LISA
We can bury it along with everything else. I'll get a shovel.

MICHAEL
(Taking a photo from her box)
Remember this? What's this Montana?

LISA
Yeah.

MICHAEL
You hair looked good like that.

LISA
It did, didn't it?

MICHAEL
Remember when we got caught in that snowstorm. And we got to
the hotel and there wasn't any heat.

LISA
Wearing our coats to bed. The tractor trailer on the side of the road
like a dinosaur.

MICHAEL
On its side.

LISA
Yeah.

MICHAEL
And we were so cold but we took off all our clothes and piled the
coats on top of the blankets.

LISA
We had to.

MICHAEL
And made love.

LISA
I remember.

MICHAEL
It was like our bodies were made for each other.

LISA
I know. It was so cold.

MICHAEL
We kept each other warm.

(And then they are kissing. They tear at each other's clothes.)

(Blackout)

Scene 2

(The apartment is as we left it. MICHAEL and LISA are wearing fewer clothes. They are post-coital.)

MICHAEL
That was good.

LISA
Yeah. OK. So let's finish.

MICHAEL
Finish?

LISA
The funeral.

MICHAEL
Oh, you—

LISA
What, you think—

MICHAEL
I mean, yeah. I do. You don't?

LISA
I don't know. I mean you have a new apartment don't you?
Wheels are in motion.

MICHAEL
I don't really have a place. I'm just staying on Brian's couch.

LISA
Oh.

MICHAEL
I just said I had a place.

LISA
Oh.

MICHAEL
To make it easier.

LISA
So you don't—

MICHAEL
I mean I could stay.

LISA
Wait, hold on. Hold on. Just because we made love doesn't mean everything's OK.

MICHAEL
I know.

LISA
Do you know?

MICHAEL
No, I mean, I though it meant everything was OK.

LISA
Right. It's not. I'm still angry at you.

MICHAEL
I'm angry at you too.

LISA
Right now?

MICHAEL
No, not right now, but in theory.

LISA
But things are not OK. You understand?

MICHAEL
Yes. OK. No. I mean. Things are better, though, right?

LISA
Maybe a little. But we need to talk. I need to tell you —

MICHAEL
I need to tell you too.

LISA
OK, we'll tell each other. And counseling. Yes?

MICHAEL
Okay.

LISA
So. Right. OK, you can come back. On a trial basis.

MICHAEL
You too. On a trial basis.

LISA
As for the funeral . . .

MICHAEL
Well it was a false alarm. The body sat bolt upright in the coffin.
There's life left after all.

LISA
OK. We'll postpone the funeral.

MICHAEL
Right.

LISA
It's a postponement. Because the relationship may not be dead.
But it's fragile. It'll need work. It's not quite healthy. You will
have to—

MICHAEL
You too.

LISA
OK, me too.

MICHAEL
I'm glad.

LISA
I am too.

MICHAEL
Want to help me unpack?

LISA
Not really. I have to go back to work. I just want to make sure
you didn't take any of my stuff.

MICHAEL
I'm glad you were here.

LISA
Me too.

(They kiss. She exits. He starts to unpack the box.)

Snow
Copyright © 2019, Adam Szymkowicz

Seth Glewen
The Gersh Agency
41 Madison Avenue 33rd Floor
New York, NY 10010
P: 212-997-1818
F: 212-391-8459
sglewen@gershny.com

SPECIAL NOTE

performances of the Play and in all instances in which the title of the Play appears for purposes of advertising, publicizing, or otherwise exploiting the Play and/or a production thereof. The name of the Author must appear on a separate line, in which no other name appears, immediately beneath the title and in size of type equal to 50% of the size of the largest, most prominent letter used for the title of the Play. No person, firm, or entity may receive credit larger or more prominent than that of the Author.

Snow
by Adam Szymkowicz

CHUCK--male
ED-- male
FRANKIE--female
SARA--female

(ED in spot)

ED

I've been careful, always very careful. Before touching a woman I
put on rubber gloves. Some women are taken aback sure, when
you pull out rubber gloves and dental dams but what kinds of
women are those?—women that know they have diseases. And
those are not the type of women I want to know in any case. So
when people ask me if I'm upset at being a virgin at my age, I say
no way.

I'm just looking for a clean woman. I am not against kissing—I
just want to make sure her mouth is well cleaned first. If she
would brush her teeth and then gargle with mouthwash for a
minimum of sixty seconds. I, of course would also brush and
mouthwash. I like cleanliness, that's all. We are all dirty. God
knows I scrub my hands before putting those rubber gloves on.

(SARA in spot)

SARA

I've been careful, always very careful. Sure there are people who
leave the house more than I do. They take strolls, they cross
streets in the midst of traffic. They get on airplanes and fly
halfway across the world. And I say good for them. If they want
to risk their lives daily, let em. But don't ask me to. I'm fine how
I am. It is true I have not left my apartment in three years.
Everyone delivers in New York. Everyone. My mother says I
would meet more people if I left my apartment—but I have my
college friends I still call and email and of course there is a large

online community waiting to hear my every word. Anyway, people die when they take risks. I've seen it happen.

(FRANKIE and CHUCK in a bar, looking out the window)

FRANKIE

It's nice to just sit here and watch the snow.

CHUCK

Yeah.

FRANKIE

It's very beautiful. Calming in a way, if you're not watching the people try to get rid of it.

CHUCK

Uh huh.

FRANKIE

There's something institutional about snow, don't you agree?

CHUCK

I hadn't noticed.

FRANKIE

It's definitely the most institutional precipitation. Take for example how afraid of it people are.

CHUCK

People aren't afraid of snow.

FRANKIE

They would lock it up and put it on tranquilizers if they could. Instead, what do we do? We salt it. We melt it, push it away. Get that away from me. Not that—not snow! Put it on a truck! Get it the hell out of here! It's not melting fast enough. Destroy it! Destroy it before it destroys us! We live in a very Puritanical society still.

                        CHUCK
I guess so.

                        FRANKIE
What's wrong?

                        CHUCK
Nothing. It's just . . . That woman I deliver to—the one who
never leaves her apartment. Something she said today really
depressed me.

                        FRANKIE
What?

                        CHUCK
I don't even know why really. It was so small.

                        FRANKIE
What'd she say?

                        CHUCK
She said—

                        SARA
I don't know, Chuck. I hope you're doing what you like. Most of
us never have the chance to be what we want to be.

                        CHUCK
And it just made me realize. I don't really even want to be inside
this body. There are so many people I would rather be.

                        FRANKIE
Like me?

                        CHUCK
Absolutely, I'd like to be you. I'd like to be inside you and I don't
just mean have sex with you which is something I also want as I'm
sure you know, but I want to know what it feels like inside you.

Like if I touch this and you touch this I know what it feels like
when I touch it but I have no idea what you feel when you touch it.
That's minor. But for example, what do you dream? You can tell
me about them and try to describe them but I'll never really know
what you see. And that's just the start of the problem because
really what I want is to be everybody.

                              FRANKIE
Everybody?

                              CHUCK
Well, especially attractive women.

                              FRANKIE
I'm not going to have sex with you, Chuck.

                              CHUCK
I know.

                              FRANKIE
Chuck, look at me. You and I will never have sex.

                              CHUCK
Never?

                              FRANKIE
Never.

                              CHUCK
Are you sure?

                              FRANKIE
Positive.

                              CHUCK
I think I should go.

                              FRANKIE
Because I won't have sex with you?

                    CHUCK
I'm feeling kind of vulnerable right now.

                    FRANKIE
I'm sorry.

                    CHUCK
It's OK. I should go.

                    FRANKIE
You going to at least finish your drink?

                              (CHUCK downs the rest of
                              his drink.)

                    FRANKIE
See you soon.

                    CHUCK
Yeah, whatever.

                    FRANKIE
Shit!

                              (FRANKIE sits there quietly
                              for a few moments. ED walks
                              in)

                    FRANKIE
Ed. Hey, Ed. Over here!

                    ED
Oh hey Frankie.

                    FRANKIE
How's it going?

                    ED
Good. Good.

                                        FRANKIE
That's really good.

                                        ED
Yeah. Yeah.

                                        FRANKIE
I just had a fight with my friend Chuck.

                                        ED
Sorry to hear that.

                                        FRANKIE
I told him I wouldn't have sex with him.

                                        ED
Oh.

                                        FRANKIE
It's not that I don't find him attractive. I mean you know Chuck.

                                        ED
Sure.

                                        FRANKIE
And it's not that I'm not in the mood. Or I was but then I was
trying to tell him something about the snow and he just blew me
off. Anyway, every time I have sex with someone I'm friends
with, we don't end up being friends after that.

                                        ED
Right.

                                        FRANKIE
You know what I'm saying?

                                        ED
I do.

                              FRANKIE

The real problem is, however, I have a nagging feeling I am
incapable of love. There was a time when it was ever possible. I
thought every day *today I will fall in love*. But that never
happened. Occasionally I fell into like but never love. I must be
broken. What's wrong with me?

                                ED

Nothing.

                              FRANKIE

I would probably be fine if I just never believed in it. Why did I
have to be born such a fucking romantic?

                                ED

Dunno.

                              FRANKIE

Why can't sex be enough? Why am I searching for this thing that
if I find it, I'm not even sure I'll recognize it anyway? I guess I
believe there's something more out there-that one person I'll find
one day. So there's no point in having sex with Chuck. He's not
the one.

                                ED

Yeah.

                              FRANKIE

How's your sex life, Ed?

                                ED

It's slow, to be honest, Frankie. It's slow. In fact not moving at all.
You could say non- existent, honestly. Having never moved
anywhere. Stalled in the driveway.

                              FRANKIE

Snowed in.

                                ED

You could say that. I feel like I'm missing everything.

                    FRANKIE
You're not.

                    ED
But I am.

                    FRANKIE
You'll find that special someone.

                    ED
I think I already did but I messed it up.

                    FRANKIE
I'm sure you didn't mess it up.

                    ED
I asked her to douche.

                    FRANKIE
Oh.

                    ED
Things kind of went downhill from there. And I'm not saying she
was a perfect person. She never left her apartment and she wasn't
always cognizant of cleanliness to the degree I would like. But I
think we understood each other for a time. I remember she said
once —

                    SARA
There are many things I do not understand although I am an
intelligent person. There are things beyond my grasp—things that
screech or howl out numbers. There are darknesses I cannot
comprehend. There is death somewhere and somewhere black
holes and tears in our unconscious.

Somehow the brain works but how I couldn't tell you. One day
my heart will stop and so will yours but at this moment we sit
beside each other with our beating hearts and our pleasant faces.

We are afraid, you and I. We are terrified people. Many people aren't as terrified as we are. They slip through life without concerns or wants. They don't worry about what they know but instead they purchase things and eat up every new TV program. These people are happy and perhaps we should be more like them. But we are not and no one can control the weather.

Try as we might we are only these creatures with two legs, maybe a soul, some of us a God, all of us hearts beating until they don't. And I will stay here with you because it is what I want. I think it is what you want too. And we will work towards some design perhaps or maybe just screw but either way I will be happy for more than a few moments and maybe someday when we are old, we will sit holding hands looking out the window at the snow falling.

                    FRANKIE
She sounds great.

                      ED
She is. Sometimes. I mean we had problems. I dunno. I haven't seen her in a while. Maybe I should go on some kind of drug.

                    FRANKIE
Can you go back and apologize?

                      ED
I don't know.

                    (CHUCK reenters.)

                    CHUCK
I'm sorry I left like that. I'm a mother fucker. Oh, hey Ed.

                      ED
Hey.

                    FRANKIE
I'm sorry too.

                                CHUCK
But are you really sure we will never have sex?

                                FRANKIE
I don't know. I guess anything can happen, but mostly I'm sure.

                                CHUCK
Yeah, I mean I guess I knew that. It's a shame, though.

                                FRANKIE
Be that as it may….

                                ED
Maybe I should call her up. Say something to her. What would I
say? I'm really messed up.

                                CHUCK
What's going on?

                                ED
Nothing.

                                FRANKIE
You should go find her.

                                ED
I don't have to find her. I know where she is.

                                FRANKIE
You should go there.

                                ED
Uh huh.

                                FRANKIE
Right now.

                                ED
I know.

                            FRANKIE
You owe it to yourself and to her too.

                            ED
I know.

                            FRANKIE
Did you love her?

                            ED
I did.

                            CHUCK
You gotta go to her then.

                            ED
I know.

                            CHUCK
Before it's too late.

                            ED
I know.

                            CHUCK
Before she finds someone else.

                            ED
I should go.

                            FRANKIE
Are you going to go?

                            ED
I don't think so. No, I don't think so.

                            (Pause.)

                        FRANKIE
Look at the snow. It's very beautiful, don't you think?

                        ED
Yeah.

                        CHUCK
It is.

                        *(SARA in her apartment also
                        looks out at the snow.)*

Seth Glewen
The Gersh Agency
41 Madison Avenue 33rd Floor
New York, NY 10010
P: 212-997-1818
F: 212-391-8459
sglewen@gershny.com

SPECIAL NOTE

with performances of the Play and in all instances in which the title of the Play appears for purposes of advertising, publicizing, or otherwise exploiting the Play and/or a production thereof. The name of the Author must appear on a separate line, in which no other name appears, immediately beneath the title and in size of type equal to 50% of the size of the largest, most prominent letter used for the title of the Play. No person, firm, or entity may receive credit larger or more prominent than that of the Author.

Golden Town
by Adam Szymkowicz

*(A fantastic Seuss-like land. The narrators are colorful and play
many roles.)*

LUCY

PERSON 1

PERSON 2

PERSON 3

1
In Golden Town
Above the ground
Little Lucy Brown was born

3
Lucy was a special child
As special as special could be
She was smart
She was kind
She was mechanically inclined

2
But when she was young
Poor little Lucy
They all had fun
At her expense

(3, 2 and 1 become children and push LUCY around.)

3
You're a dork

2
You're a geek

1
You're a dweeb

3
You're a freak

2
You're a bore

1
A whore

3
Your parents are poor

2
You have the clap.

1
What's that?

3
Lucy cried and ran away
She ran to hide
Covered her eyes
Found a barrel and climbed inside

1, 2, 3
And there she stayed for thirteen years.

1
When she emerged all those years later, she did not recognize
Golden Town

LUCY
Is this my home?
Is this my town?

2
On the stone roads
She walked around

3
Her hair had turned from green to brown.

2
Her eyes, twice the size

1
When she grew in Golden Town

3
The townies surrounded her to see who--

2
--what she was

1
Who is this?

3
What is she?

2
What's the story?

3
What's the buzz?

LUCY
I'm Lucy. I'm here.
To ease all your fears.
To heal you.
(Aside.) To exact revenge.

I'm Lucy. I'm glad.
For the time I've had

For the thoughts I've thunk
For thirteen years

1
Who is she?

2
Do you know her?

3
Is she the one we've been waiting for?

1
Is she the savior?

2
Is she the poet?

3
Has she come to open the door?

2
And they led her down the path.

3
Past the bar, the public bath

1
Over the hill, beside the tree

2
Beyond the rock

3
Beside the sea

1
And there was the door no Golden Townie could open.

2
The locksmiths had all tried

3
And the strongmen and the guys

1
With chisels and hammers

2
Dynamite and slammers

3
Picks and sticks

1
Nails and kicks

2
But none could open the door.

3
But Lucy had come from where God knows.

2
Could she open it?

1
Could she do it, you suppose?

LUCY
I'll make you a deal.

1
Said Lucy. What gall!

LUCY
If I open the door give me one small . . .

2
Anything

3
The people swore

1,2,3
We must know what's behind that door.

LUCY
You'll give me whatever I want?

1
Anything within reason.

2
All the fruit in season.

3
All the pigs we got

1
All the wine and pot

LUCY
All I want is my name in the book

1,2,3
The book?!

LUCY
As the girl who did it
The girl who opened the door

1
Is that all?

2
No pot?

3
Do it and we'll give that and more

1
The light and the dark

2
Love in the park

3
And all the candy from the store

LUCY
Come back tomorrow and I'll see what I can do

1
All night she stood before the door

2
She tapped and she pushed, shoved and slapped

3
She jiggled the lock
Wiggled the knob
Giggled, cried
Wriggled and sobbed

1
She refused to give up
Though the sun was about to rise
She knew she had to act
Before all her brags turned to lies

LUCY
I should be able to do this
I'm really quite a find
I'm smart and I'm able
And mechanically inclined

3
But the sun was about to rise
The door loomed
before her eyes
Twice the size

LUCY
Why won't you open?
What must I do?
I've been working for years
To improve myself
I'm at the top of my game
I've got wisdom and health
And if it's all the same
I'd like you to open
What must I do?
What must I do?

2
Then the door replied
Sounds too fantastic?
You'll think I lied
But it spoke to little Lucy
Now grown
It said
It's commonly known
I only open
For one special person

LUCY
That's me
I'm as special
As special can be.

1
This person
Said the door
Must really want in
Must need
With greed

Approaching sin
Must desire
Must be driven
By an inner fire

2
To succeed

LUCY
But that's me
Don't you see?

I've got to get you open
Get my name in the book
Thirteen years of childhood
It's time they take a look
At who they cast away

Lucy Brown is back in town
And she's going to be a great success

3
And Lucy pulled one last time
With all that she had
Every ounce of need
Until her hands
began to bleed

1
And the door began to creak

2
And moan

3
It shrieked

1
And groaned

2
And finally opened wide

(LUCY opens door.)

3
As the townies climbed the mountainside

1
They saw Lucy open the door

LUCY
I'm Lucy Brown

1
She said

LUCY
I was born in Golden Town
Put my name in the book
I'm the one who opened the door
I'm not a dork or a geek
A dweeb or a freak
I'm not a whore or a bore
I'm the great opener

2
And with that she shut the door behind her

3
And the townies couldn't find her

1
And she became a legend in the book

2
They say the door never opened again

3
Though the townies all tried

2
With the sticks and the picks

3
Hammers and slammers

1
They all tried to get inside

2
But what about you? If Lucy can do it, why don't you try?

(Curtain.)

Printed in Great Britain
by Amazon